Introduction

For over thirty years, visitors to my office have been delighted and intrigued by the number of illustrated envelopes arranged in frames on the walls. Recently, two members of the wonderful Random House sales team, Kate Gunning and Peter Fry, urged me to put them into print. My dear friend David McKee started things off many years ago with the first envelope; this was soon followed by more. I proudly displayed these in my office and they inspired contributions from other artists and friends including Satoshi Kitamura and Fulvio Testa.

I now have more than 200 envelopes, some of which have featured in *Graphis Magazine*. Others have been exhibited at the Japanese Post Office Museum and in the showrooms of Peters Library Suppliers in Birmingham. The art of letter-writing is in danger of dying out, I am sorry to say; all the more reason, then, for celebrating that art in this little book. These are also challenging times for the printed book, but I sincerely hope and believe that picture books will continue to be enjoyed and shared for many generations to come.

Publisher, Andersen Press

All proceeds from the sales of this book will be donated to Save the Children.

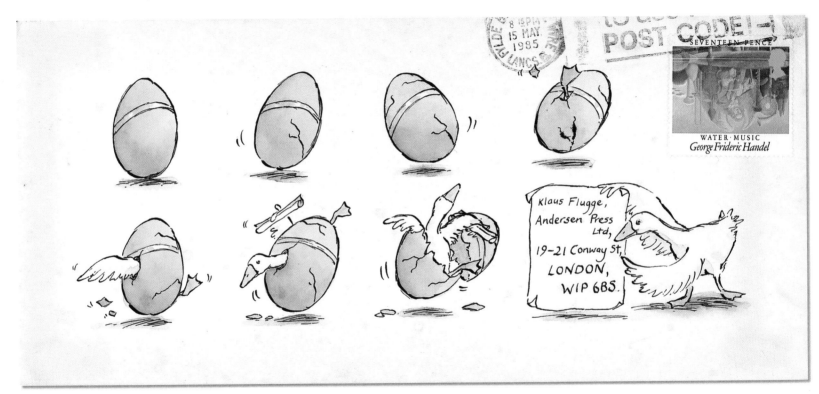

Susan Varley

Philippe Dupasquier

REMEMBER
POST COD
KLAUS FLUGGE
ANDERSEN PRESS
3 FITZROY SQUARE
LONDON W1

David McKee

KLAUS FLUGGE, ⒶNDERSEN PRESS, 20 VAUXHALL BRIDGE ROAD, LONDON SW1V 2SA.

Philippe Dupasquier

KLAUS FLÜGGE, ANDERSEN PRESS, 20 VAUXHALL BRIDGE Rd, LONDON SW1V2SA Angleterre

David McKee

Klaus Flugge
Andersen Press Ltd
3. Fitzroy Square
London W1 P GJDL

16P   Highland Cow

Ralph Steadman

KLAUS FLUGGE
ANDERSEN PRESS
20 VAUXHALL
BRIDGE ROAD
LONDON
SW1V 2SA

Satoshi Kitamura

KLAUS FLUGGE ANDERSEN PRESS 20 VAUXHALL BRIDGE

LONDON SWIV2JA

ENGLAND

00122X0001

Fulvio Testa

KLAUS FLÜGGE, ANDERSEN PRESS, 20, VAUXHALL BRIDGE ROAD, LONDON S.W.1 V 2 SA
Angleterre

David McKee

David McKee

KLAUS FLUGGE
ANDERSEN PRESS
20 VAUXHALL BRIDGE ROAD
LONDON S·W I V 2SA
ANGLETERRE

David McKee

Klaus Flugge
ANDERSEN PRESS
20 VAUXHALL BRIDGE ROAD
LONDON
SW1V 2SA

SATOSHI

Satoshi Kitamura

KLAUS FLUGGE
ANDERSEN PRESS
62-65 CHANDOS PLACE
COVENT GARDEN W.C.2.

HAPPY BIRTHDAY KLAUS

1ST

David McKee

David McKee

David McKee

Satoshi Kitamura

David McKee

Max Velthuijs

David McKee

KLAUS FLUGGE, (A)NDERSEN PRESS, 20 VAUXHALL BRIDGE ROAD LONDON SW1V 2SA

Philippe Dupasquier

Philippe Dupasquier

Philippe Dupasquier

Fulvio Testa

Satoshi Kitamura

Susan Varley

KLAUS FLUGGE
ANDERSEN PRESS
3 FITZROY SQUARE
LONDON W1
ENGLAND.

David McKee

Tony Ross

David McKee

David McKee

David McKee

2000

2001

06 NICE CTC
27.12.00 2 in
ALPES MARITIMES

liberté
égalité
fraternité
LA POSTE

Klaus Flügge, Andersen Press, 20 Vauxhall Bridge Road
LONDON S.W.1 2USA Angleterre

David McKee

Klaus Flugge
ANDERSEN PRESS
20 Vauxhall Bridge Rd
LONDON SW1V 2SA
Angleterre.

David McKee

Klaus Flugge
Andersen Press
3 Fitzroy Square
London WI P 6JD

David McKee

Klaus Fluggl
Andersen Press
20 Vauxhall Bridge Rd
LONDON S.W1
ANGLETERRE

David McKee

David McKee

First Class

KLAUS FLUGGE
ANDERSEN PRESS
20 VAUXHALL BRIDGE ROAD
LONDON SW1V 2SA

Satoshi Kitamura

David McKee

Klaus Flugge
19~21 Conway Street
London W1P 5HL

Philippe Matter

David McKee

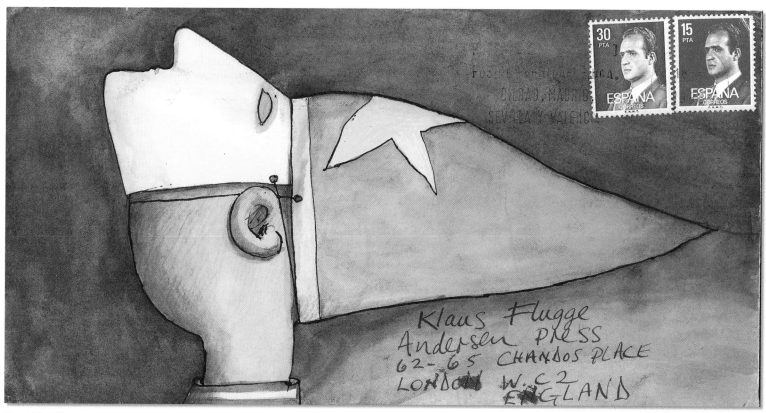

David McKee

David McKee

David McKee

David McKee

Klaus Flügge
Andersen Press
20 Vauxhall Bridge Road
LONDON
SW1V 2SA

David McKee

Satoshi Kitamura

David McKee

David McKee

David McKee

ANDERSEN PRESS

KLAUS FLUGGE
20 VAUXHALL
BRIDGE ROAD
LONDON
SW1V 2SA

22P

Satoshi Kitamura

Philippe Dupasquier

Satoshi Kitamura

KLAUS FLUGGE
ANDERSEN PRESS
20 VAUXHALL BRIDGE ROAD
LONDON SW1 V 2SA
ENGLAND

David McKee

David McKee

ANDERSEN · PRESS · LIMITED.

Mr KLAUS FLÜGGE

62/65 Chandos Place, Covent Garden

LONDON WC2N 4NW GRANDE BRETAGNE

Frédéric Joos

David McKee

Susan Varley

David McKee

Satoshi Kitamura

TONBRIDGE
6 45PM
2 JLY
1997
KENT

Please control
your dog
when the
postman calls

26
Dracula

Klaos Flugge
Andersen Press LTD
20 Vauxhall Bridge Road
LONDON SW1V 2SA

Philippe Dupasquier

Klaus Flügge,
Andersen PRESS,
20 Vauxhall Bridge Rd.,
LONDON S.W1 V2SA
Angleterre

David McKee

Philippe Dupasquier

David McKee

Klaus Flugge
ANDERSEN PRESS
20 VAUXHALL BRIDGE ROAD
LONDON SW1V 2SA

Satoshi Kitamura

Klaus Flügge, Andersen Press   20. Vauxhall Bridge Road LONDON
S.W1V 2SA
Angleterre

David McKee

Satoshi Kitamura

KLAUS FLUGGE. @ ANDERSEN PRESS, 20 VAUXHALL BRIDGE ROAD. LONDON SW1V 2SA

Philippe Dupasquier

Susan Varley

Posy Simmonds

KLAUS FLUGGE
ANDERSEN PRESS
19-21 CONWAY STREET
LONDON W1P 6JD

Tony Ross

Klaus Flügge, Andersen PRESS 20 Vauxhall Bridge Road LONDON SW1V 2SA Angleterre

David McKee

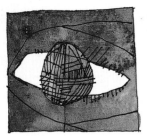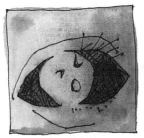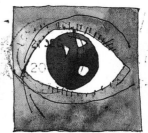

Klaus Flugge Andersen Press 20 Vauxhall Bridge Road London SW1V 2SA

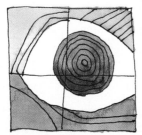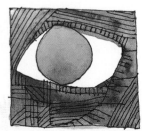

Satoshi Kitamura

David McKee

Tony Ross

Satoshi Kitamura

Satoshi Kitamura

David McKee

Satoshi Kitamura

Klaus Flügge, Andersen Press, 20 Vauxhall Bridge Rd, London SW1V 2S.
O.K.

Fiona Moodie

Satoshi Kitamura

Max Velthuijs

Klaus Flugge ANDERSEN PRESS 20 Vauxhall BRIDGE Road LONDON SW1V 2SA

Satoshi Kitamura

Mr Klaus Flugge,
Andersen Press,
20 Vauxhall Bridge
Road,
London SW1 V2SA

Emma Chichester Clark

KLAUS FLUGGE . ⒶNDERSEN PRESS . 20 VAUXHALL BRIDGE ROAD . LONDON . SW1.2SA

Philippe Dupasquier

Susan Varley

David McKee

Fulvio Testa

David McKee

First Class

KLAUS FLUGGE ANDERSEN PRESS
62-65 Chandos Place
COVENT GARDEN
LONDON WC2N 4NW

Satoshi Kitamura

Tony Ross

Satoshi Kitamura

Klaus Flügge
Andersen Press
20 Vauxhall Bridge Road
LONDON S.W.1 V2SA

Angleterre

David McKee

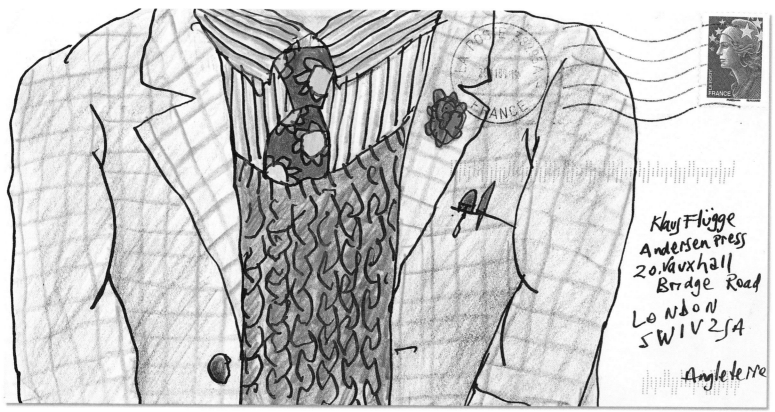

David McKee

Chris Riddell

Susan Varley

Satoshi Kitamura

Frédéric Joos

Susan Varley

Tony Ross

David McKee   Axel Scheffler

Klaus Flugge

Klaus Flugge was born in Germany in 1934. After training as a bookseller in Leipzig, he became a refugee and worked in Hamburg, emigrating to the USA in 1957. He joined Abelard-Schuman in New York, later transferring to London as a publisher of adult and children's books. He commissioned work from artists such as Edward Ardizzone, Quentin Blake, Michael Foreman, David McKee and Ralph Steadman.

In 1976, Klaus launched his own publishing company, Andersen Press (named after Hans Christian Andersen), with picture books from, among others, Ruth Brown, Philippe Dupasquier, Leo Lionni and Tony Ross. Since then, there have been more than 2000 titles for children by the likes of Michael Foreman, Satoshi Kitamura, David McKee and Emma Chichester Clark. The fiction list includes prize-winning work by Melvin Burgess and Jason Wallace. Andersen Press is responsible for such modern classics as *I Want My Potty!* by Tony Ross and *Badger's Parting Gifts* by Susan Varley. Probably the best-known character of all is *Elmer the Patchwork Elephant*, created by David McKee.

In 1999 Klaus received the Eleanor Farjeon Award for his outstanding contribution to children's books. In 2010 he became only the second publisher to be awarded honorary membership of the Youth Libraries Group.